*Efner Tudor Holmes*

# AMY'S GOOSE

*illustrated by Tasha Tudor*

HarperTrophy

*A Division of* HarperCollins*Publishers*

*Library of Congress Cataloging-in-Publication Data*
Holmes, Efner Tudor.
Amy's goose.
SUMMARY: Amy nurses a wild goose back to
health and struggles to decide whether to keep it
on the farm or let it be free.
[1. Geese—Fiction.   2. Farm life—Fiction]
I. Tudor, Tasha.   II. Title. PZ7.H735Am      [E]      77-3027
ISBN 0-690-03800-3
ISBN 0-690-03801-1 (lib. bdg.)
ISBN 0-06-443091-X (pbk.)

*For a very special person,*
*Jeanette Holmes*
*…more lovingly known as*
*Great Grammie*

Amy stood in the garden watching the sun sink behind the hills. She had been helping her parents dig the last of the potatoes. The air smelled of cool damp earth mixed with the scent of the gold and orange leaves that fell silently and incessantly to the ground.

Then Amy heard the cry she had been waiting for all fall.

Her face turned eagerly to the sky, and she saw the long V of the wild geese. Their call was faint at first, then louder as they flew closer. The cry fell down to her, carrying with it the spirit of all wild things. The geese began to break their formation as they came near the lake at the edge of the potato field. Amy knew that they would settle there for the night. They always did and she had a large sack of corn in the barn, all ready for them. Usually a flock would settle at night and by daybreak be off again on its long journey south. Many times, in other years, Amy had seen the geese rise up through the morning mist. They

would circle aimlessly for a moment and then the great long V
would take shape and Amy would watch them as they flew
away. In her mind, she could still hear their cry. To her, they
seemed to be calling good-bye and she would be filled with
loneliness. For Amy was an only child and the wild creatures
were her friends.

But now the geese were over her, and coming in low. They
were so close that Amy could feel the wind from their great
white wings. She stood, a small, still figure, as the geese flew past
her and landed in the lake and on its shores.

Someone called to her and she turned to see her father walking down the garden. He stood beside her and put an arm around her shoulders.

"Well, little one," he said, "I see your friends have come back. As soon as we get these potatoes under cover and eat dinner we'll get that sack of corn."

"Aren't they beautiful?" Amy asked him. "And there are a lot more of them this year."

Her father grinned down at her.

"That's because they've been spreading the word about a lake where a little girl will be waiting with a hundred pounds of good corn," he teased her. "Now come, it's almost dark and we've got to get these potatoes in."

Dinner seemed to Amy to be taking unusually long. Ordinarily she loved sitting there in the dining room with all three of them together, and the candles casting soft shadows on the warm wood-paneled walls. The room smelled of freshly baked apple and pumpkin pies. But Amy's thoughts were with the geese out on the moonlit lake. *Her* geese, she thought. They had remembered, and had come back to her again! She could hardly wait to go out to them, and to bring them some corn. It was a ritual she had kept up since one fall when the snow came early and some geese had stayed longer than usual. Amy had felt sorry for them and worried that they wouldn't have enough to eat. So she had scattered corn for them.

At last her father pushed back his chair and stood up. Amy got her sweater and followed him out to the barn. He hoisted the sack of corn to his shoulder and together Amy and her father walked down through the garden and into the field by the lake. The stillness of the night was broken only by the crickets singing their lonely song of the end of summer.

All at once they heard the frantic honking of a goose. Then the flock began to pick up its cry and Amy could hear their wings beating on the water. As she ran down the field she saw many geese rising up into the air in confusion and fright. Others stayed on the shore, standing with their long necks stretched low to the ground as they gabbled in alarm.

"It's a fox," her father cried. "Look, he's got one." Dropping the sack of corn he picked up a rock and flung it at the fox. Amy ran at him clapping her hands and yelling. The fox let go

of the goose and fled. But the goose lay still. On its white neck
Amy saw a spreading spot of blood. She kneeled down and, as
gently as she could, she picked up the big bird. The frightened
goose beat its wings and tried to fly away but it was too feeble to
struggle for long. Soon it lay quietly, its wings drooped over
Amy's legs and onto the sand. Amy's father squatted down to
look.

"It may not really be as bad as it looks," he said. "I think we
can save her. Let's get her up to the barn."

He lifted the goose from Amy's arms and they headed back up the field. Amy turned once to look toward the lake. All was quiet again and Amy saw several geese nibbling at the sack of corn they had forgotten on the shore.

When Amy went to look at the wounded goose the next morning, she was surprised to see it standing up and pecking at a dish of feed. But it was obviously still in some pain. Amy went slowly into the pen. She held out her hand but the goose hissed at her fiercely and retreated to a far corner. So the goose and the girl sat for several minutes regarding each other.

"It's all right," Amy said softly. "You're safe here."

Amy spent most of the rest of the day with the goose. That evening the wild creature ate a few grains of corn from her hand. And when she stroked its head, the goose would gabble in what Amy felt sure was affection. A very special feeling for the big white bird was growing in her. She wondered hopefully if she'd be able to tame it. Amy thought it would be a real gift to have this wild bird place its trust in her.

For several days Amy was so busy taking care of her goose that she didn't stop to think it strange that the other geese had not left the lake to continue their journey to the warm South. One late afternoon Amy and the white goose were out on the lawn. Amy was eating an apple and giving bits of it to the goose. Suddenly they heard the cry of a goose overhead. Amy looked up to see a lone bird flying over the barn. It would circle silently,

then start up its cry. Amy's goose stood listening intently, with her head cocked to one side, looking up into the sky at the other bird. Then she began answering his call and flapping her wings. She ran over to Amy and nibbled at a piece of apple, but then she stood listening again. On the lake, Amy saw the rest of the flock. They had not left! They were waiting for her goose…and that must be her mate calling to her!

"Come on," she said to the goose, "I'm going to shut you up. You're not strong enough for flying yet. Next spring they'll be back."

Amy put the goose in its pen in the barn, closed the door firmly, and went to help her mother fix dinner. But all evening she felt upset. The warm house seemed to hold her in, like a cage. She thought of her goose, of the wild creature she had shut in the barn. She knew that the goose *was* really well enough for the long flight now. And she thought of the white gander flying alone over the barn calling to his mate.

She slipped out of the house and went through the shadow-filled garden and down to the lake. It was a cold night and mist was drifting up from the lake into the moonlight. Amy felt an eerie restlessness. Then she saw the geese. They, too, were restless. Several of them would rise up and call to the others, then drop back into the water. Others stood clustered on the shore as if holding a meeting.

Suddenly, they all rose up into the sky together. Their farewell cry filled the air and Amy watched them fall into flight formation. She would see no more geese until spring. Winter was coming. Amy knew it and obviously the geese sensed it, too. The flock had already grown small in the distant sky when Amy saw a lone bird drop out and begin flying back. Amy knew where it was headed.

She began running up the field. As she came to the barn, she heard the cry of the lone gander in the cold air and then the muffled honking that answered him from the barn. She flung open the door and ran to the pen where she had put her goose. The white goose was frantically pushing against the wire. When

she saw Amy she stretched out her long neck and gabbled. Amy kneeled down. She put her arms around the big bird, and the goose put her beak in the curve of Amy's neck. Amy began to cry. She held the bird tightly, wishing it could stay. Then she picked up the white bird and carried her out into the night.

They stood silently together for a moment, until the goose set up a cry and began to run and beat her wings. Amy could hear the gander answering and as she watched, the goose rose into the moonlight. Her mate joined her and together they flew, following the flock before them.

Amy stood alone in the night and wiped away her tears. She felt the cold ground under her bare feet and thought of Spring, when she would be standing by the lake watching a flock of white geese fly over her and into the water.